This book belongs to

....

First published in 2014 by Miles Kelly Publishing Ltd
Harding's Barn, Bardfield End Green, Thaxted, Essex, CM6 3PX, UK

2 4 6 8 10 9 7 5 3 1

Publishing Director Belinda Gallagher
Creative Director Jo Cowan
Editor Fran Bromage
Senior Designer Joe Jones
Production Manager Elizabeth Collins
Reprographics Stephan Davis, Jennifer Hunt, Thom Allaway

ISBN 978-1-78209-491-3

Printed in China

British Library Cataloguing-in-Publication Data
A catalogue record for this book is available from the British Library

ACKNOWLEDGEMENTS

The publishers would like to thank the following artists
who have contributed to this book:

Cover (main): Hannah Wood at Advocate Art
Insides: Elizabeth Sawyer

Made with paper from a sustainable forest

www.mileskelly.net   info@mileskelly.net

Hansel and Gretel

Miles Kelly

Once upon a time, a poor woodcutter and his cruel wife lived near a forest. The woodcutter had two children, Hansel and Gretel. One day,

Hansel and Gretel

Hansel heard his stepmother say to his father, "There are too many mouths to feed. You must leave the children in the forest tomorrow."

The father didn't want to abandon his children, but his wife insisted. Hansel's heart grew icy cold, but he was a clever boy, so after dark he slipped out of the house and filled his pockets with shiny white stones.

The next morning the children followed their father deep into the forest. Hansel

dropped the shiny stones
all along the path.

In the forest their father lit
a fire. He told the children he
would collect more wood and
be back later. Then, he walked
home with a heavy heart.

Hansel kept their fire going
all day, but when night fell,
it grew cold. "Don't worry,"

Hansel and Gretel

Hansel told Gretel, and he led them home by moonlight, following his line of shiny white stones. Their father was overjoyed to see them, but their stepmother was not.

Some time passed, but one night, Hansel again heard his

Story time

mother demanding they be
left in the forest. But when
Hansel tried to slip away to
collect some pebbles he
found the door was locked.

In the morning, their father
gave them each a piece of
bread, and led them deeper

10

Hansel and Gretel

into the forest. Along the way,
Hansel dropped breadcrumbs
as often as he could.

After their father left,
Hansel comforted Gretel, and
they waited for the moon to
rise. But there was not a
breadcrumb to be seen. The

birds had eaten every last
one. There was nothing to do
but wait until morning.

For two days they walked
and walked, but saw nothing
but trees. They were cold,
hungry and frightened. Just
as it was getting dark again,

Hansel and Gretel

they came to a clearing. There stood a house with walls of gingerbread, windows of spun sugar and tiles made from striped sweets.

Hansel and Gretel couldn't believe their eyes, and were soon breaking off bits of the house to eat. Then a little voice said, "Nibble, nibble, little mouse. Who is that eating my sweet house?"

Out of the front door came an old woman. She smiled sweetly and said, "Dear ones, you don't need to eat my

Hansel and Gretel

house. Come inside and I'll give you lovely things to eat and warm beds to sleep in."

Hansel and Gretel needed no second asking. They were soon tucked up in cosy warm beds and full of hot milk, biscuits and apples.

Hansel and Gretel

But little did they know
they were in dreadful danger.
The old woman was a wicked
witch. She was planning to
put Gretel to work and
fatten up Hansel to eat him.
The next morning she
locked Hansel in a cage and

told Gretel to clean the whole house from top to bottom. The witch fed Hansel a huge plate of chicken. She gave Gretel a tiny, dry hunk of bread. But when the witch was asleep, Hansel shared his meal with Gretel.

Hansel and Gretel

The witch could not see very well. So, every morning she made Hansel put his finger through the bars of the cage so she could tell how fat he was getting.

But clever Hansel poked a chicken bone through the

bars so the witch thought he was still too skinny to eat. After several weeks, the witch decided to eat Hansel anyway. She made Gretel prepare the big stone oven. But Gretel pretended she couldn't reach inside the oven. As the witch bent down to help her, Gretel gave her a big shove and slammed the oven door. And that was the end of the horrid, old witch!

Gretel released Hansel from the cage, and they set off to find their way home. When they got back, their father was delighted to see them.

The poor woodcutter had been so miserable since he'd

Hansel and Gretel

taken the children to the forest, that his nasty wife had left him. And she was never seen again!

The End